To my mother, Dorothy Magnuson,
and my daughters, Kim and Kirsten —
their story.

With love
K.M.B.

In fond memory of
my Grandma Hart.

T.R.

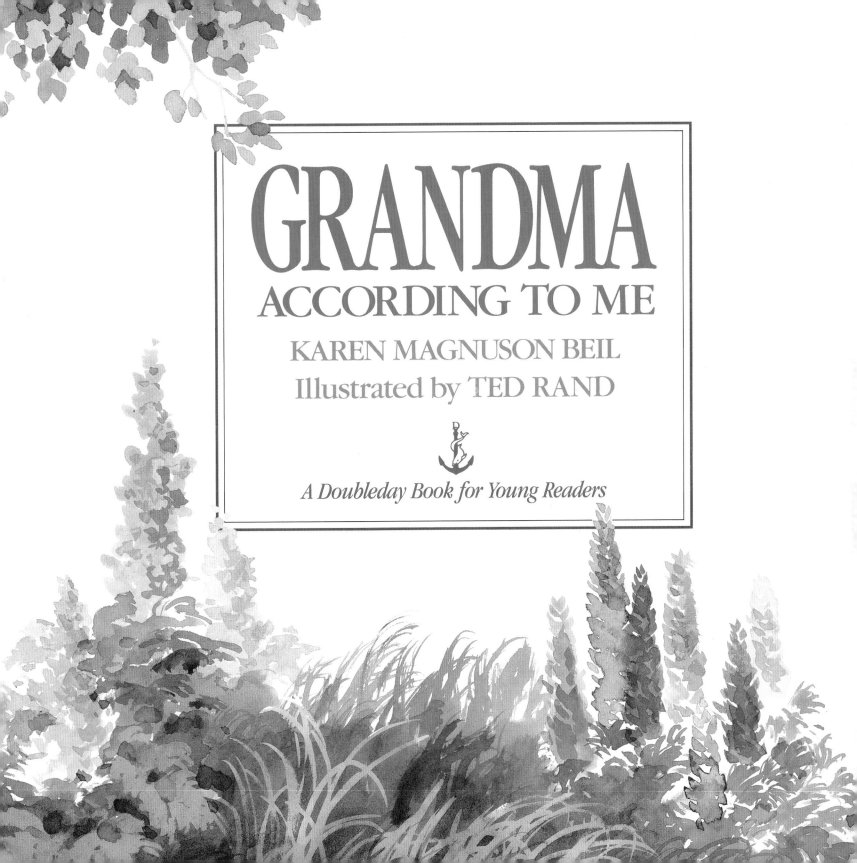

GRANDMA
ACCORDING TO ME

KAREN MAGNUSON BEIL

Illustrated by TED RAND

A Doubleday Book for Young Readers

My grandma has a lap that is big enough to hold both me and my sister—at the same time. But I like it best when it's all mine.

Grandma's lap is as soft as a pillow. There are no corners, sharp edges, or bony places that poke me while I listen to a story.

She says she's fat.
I say she's round.
She says she's plump.
I say she's comfortable.

My grandma reads me books. Her voice
is soft and low, and makes me feel good.
    She says it's deep, like dark molasses.
    I say it's sweet, like honey.

She says it's low, like Grandpa's.
I say it's like music.

My grandma bakes the best cookies in the world—and lots of them.

She says, Oops. One broke. Another reject from the cookie factory.

I say, Yum.

My grandma has a drawer in her room that I can look in anytime I want. It has rings and necklaces, little bottles of perfume, scarves, and even a slip to put on my hair when I'm pretending to be a bride.

She says it's a mess.

I say it's easier to find things that way.

She says the jewelry is fake, just colored glass and rhinestones.

But I know they're diamonds and rubies and emeralds and solid gold.

And every time I visit I get to keep one treasure from the drawer. But the drawer never gets empty.

My grandma has long fingers and can make giant, droopy bubbles with the bath soap. When I sleep at Grandma's house, we make bubbles in the tub, and we always forget to wash me.

She says, Time to get out—your hands are all wrinkly.

I say, These are my "grandma hands"—I like them this way.

But my favorite part of my grandma is her face. It has lines all over. When I was little, I used to call them "crinkles." My little sister calls them "winkles."

Grandma says they are wrinkles.

I say they are her story lines.

My grandma has a story for every single wrinkle on her face. And that's a lot of stories. Most of them come with stories about my mother when she was a little girl.

On Grandma's shelf, there are fifteen jars of creams and lotions. These are to wipe away the wrinkles. She calls them wrinkle removers.

She says, Out, out, you wrinkles, as she smears on gooey pink stuff. Then she says Abracadabra! and peeks in the mirror.

I say, Don't ever lose any. I'm glad the gooey pink stuff doesn't work.

When Grandpa gets the camera out, my grandma always turns away and hides, or pretends she needs to do something in the kitchen right away.

This many wrinkles would break the camera, she says.

Please be in the picture with me, I say. I want a picture of you and me with all our stories to keep forever.

She says, I think that I have gotten even
more wrinkles since you've been around.
   I say, That's great. Which ones are mine?
   Then Grandma smiles, and there's my answer.

ABOUT THE AUTHOR

Karen Magnuson Beil is an editor, journalist, and free-lance writer who has written extensively about conservation and environmental issues. This is her first book for children.

ABOUT THE ILLUSTRATOR

Ted Rand is a portrait painter, fine artist, and illustrator. He has illustrated such well-known books as *Knots on a Counting Rope* by Bill Martin, Jr., and John Archambault, and *Paul Revere's Ride* by Henry Wadsworth Longfellow.

ABOUT THE BOOK

The illustrations for this book were painted with Windsor Newton watercolors over drawings done with an HB pencil. The brushes used were sable and bristle for a softer edge. The boards were 100 percent rag stock, cold press number 114 Crescent.

The book is set in 18-point ITC Garamond Book Condensed, a modern cutting of the sixteenth-century classic design by Claude Garamond. The typography is by Lynn Braswell.

A Doubleday Book for Young Readers
PUBLISHED BY DELACORTE PRESS
Bantam Doubleday Dell Publishing Group, Inc.
666 Fifth Avenue, New York, New York 10103
DOUBLEDAY *and the portrayal of an anchor with a dolphin are trademarks of*
Bantam Doubleday Dell Publishing Group, Inc.

Library of Congress Cataloging in Publication Data
Beil, Karen Magnuson.
Grandma according to me / by Karen Magnuson Beil;
illustrated by Ted Rand. —
1st ed.
p.   cm.
Summary: A young girl shows how much she loves her grandmother by telling her
what she likes about her.
[1. Grandmothers—Fiction.] I. Rand, Ted, ill. II. Title.
PZ7.B3882349Wr 1992
[E]—dc20   91-10624   CIP   AC
ISBN 0-385-41484-6

RL: 2.7 / Manufactured in U.S.A. / September 1992 / 10 9 8 7 6 5 4 3 2 1 / FSL